James Sedgwick

The Law of Storms

SALZWASSER VERLAG

James Sedgwick

The Law of Storms

Reprint of the original, first published in 1856.

1st Edition 2023 | ISBN: 978-3-37517-428-6

Salzwasser Verlag is an imprint of Outlook Verlagsgesellschaft mbH.

Verlag (Publisher): Outlook Verlag GmbH, Zeilweg 44, 60439 Frankfurt, Deutschland
Vertretungsberechtigt (Authorized to represent): E. Roepke, Zeilweg 44, 60439 Frankfurt, Deutschland
Druck (Print): Books on Demand GmbH, In de Tarpen 42, 22848 Norderstedt, Deutschland

THE LAW OF STORMS.

THE TRUE PRINCIPLE

OF

THE LAW OF STORMS,

PRACTICALLY

ARRANGED FOR BOTH HEMISPHERES.

BY JAMES SEDGWICK,

FORMERLY OF THE HON. EAST INDIA COMPANY'S SERVICE, AND MANY YEARS
MASTER OF SHIPS IN THE INDIA TRADE.

" He maketh the storm a calm, so that the waves thereof are still."

Sixth Edition.

[ENTERED AT STATIONERS' HALL.]

LONDON:

PRINTED FOR THE AUTHOR;

AND SOLD BY J. D. POTTER, 31, POULTRY, AND 11, KING-STREET,
TOWER-HILL,

SOLE AGENT FOR THE ADMIRALTY CHARTS;

AND ALL NAUTICAL BOOKSELLERS.

MDCCCLVI.

PREFACE TO THE FIFTH EDITION.

My Treatise on the Law of Storms has now reached a
Fifth Edition; and so great a success on the part of my
little work seems to call for a few remarks from me.

For more than fourteen years the theory of the Law of
Storms, as a theory, was favourably received by intelligent
nautical men; but, in the course of their practical experience,
they discovered that, by assuming a given track in certain
latitudes for the progressive motion of the entire meteor, they
frequently became involved in the dangerous centre. It was
this consideration, stimulated by circumstances which I have
mentioned in the Introduction to the First Edition, that
induced me to study the subject more fully and attentively,
and to frame a set of rules, suitable to all occasions, and
calculated to prove useful even to the man who might not
thoroughly understand the theory.

I am happy to say that my brother seamen have paid me a
high compliment by the manner in which they have received
my book; and many of them have told me personally that they
completely agree with the directions which I have given
for avoiding the vortex of a storm. I feel grateful for this
encouragement; and I have carefully revised the present

edition of the work, and added a few more pages of matter, which I trust may be found useful and interesting.

Of course, I could not expect universal concurrence. It was only natural that my treatise should excite some difference of opinion. Of this I am far from complaining. I only repeat, that I entertain the most perfect confidence myself as to the accuracy of my views, and of the simple rules which I have laid down; that I am quite content to leave them to the unerring test of experience and time; and that I am only too happy to receive so much support and corroboration from my nautical brethren who speak from their practical knowledge. One of my critics, however, Mr. Piddington, of Calcutta, a theoretical speculator upon the Law of Storms, and who is the author of eighteen publications on the subject, led away by the excess of the zeal with which he appears to have become animated against my book, has insinuated that, on the occasion of the terrible hurricane in which the *Earl of Balcarras* was involved in the Mozambique Channel, in the spring of last year ('54), the ship got into difficulty on account of her commander having had the misfortune to have had my book on board, and to have followed my directions; but I am sure it will amuse my readers when I apprise them that I have a letter from Captain Morris, late commanding the *Earl of Balcarras,* informing me that he had not my book on board at all on that occasion, but that the book which he had was that of Mr. Piddington, my candid and *courteous* critic himself—a fact which I commend to Mr. Piddington's reflections. Captain Morris is good enough to add an expression of his approval of my little treatise, with which he had since become acquainted.

I have had the gratification of being informed by some, who

at the outset opposed my theory, that they have since seen reason to change their opinion, and to concur in my views. Many scientific gentlemen of eminence have conveyed to me their approval of the work. I have also to thank several of the public journals for the kind manner in which they have spoken of it. And, in addition to the support which I have received from my nautical brethren generally, I am happy to state that the *Peninsular and Oriental Steam Navigation Company* have done me the honour to stamp my book with their favourable notice.

In the autumn of 1852, Mr. R. D. Guthrie, the Nautical Superintendent of the Company, reported on my work, at the request of the Nautical Directors, and the result of that report was, that thirty copies were ordered by the Board to be distributed amongst the Company's ships. Subsequently, in December, 1853, I had the pleasure of receiving the following communication from Mr. Guthrie :—

" Peninsular and Oriental Steam Navigation Company's Offices,
122, Leadenhall-street, London, Dec. 14, 1853.

" DEAR SIR,—The Nautical Committee having had under their consideration Captain Purchase's letter, dated the 22d of May last, have desired me to forward you the following extract from it :—

(Extract from Captain Purchase's letter.)

" 'It is my opinion that we were on the N.W. verge of a severe Typhoon, but by acting according to Captain James Sedgwick's " Law of Storms," I feel satisfied we have escaped much damage.

" ' I am, &c., &c.,

" ' (Signed)   R. D. GUTHRIE.' "

In addition to the distribution of the work amongst their vessels · by the *Peninsular and Oriental Steam Navigation Company*, I have to state that the *Honourable East India Company*, also, did me the honour to order thirty copies for the use of their ships in India.

I feel that it would be superfluous to add anything to testimony of so valuable and unexceptionable a character. Approval from such quarters, and the fact that my little treatise has now reached a fifth edition, are of course very gratifying to me personally. But, far above any personal sentiments of that kind, is the hope which I entertain, · that the result will be to diffuse more widely throughout the profession what I am convinced to be the correct theory of the Law of Storms, and to afford ship-masters a sure and simple guide in escaping the disastrous effects of hurricanes.

JAMES SEDGWICK.

London, September, 1855.

ROYAL NAVY & MERCANTILE MARINE

OF

GREAT BRITAIN.

INTRODUCTION TO THE FIRST AND SUBSEQUENT EDITIONS.

THE idea of what I now consider to be the true principle of "The Law of Storms," first presented itself to my mind, in the light of conviction, on my homeward passage from the Mauritius in the latter part of 1851 and the beginning of 1852. During my short detention at the Mauritius in December, 1851, about twenty vessels put in, more or less dismasted. The quantity of damaged cargo landed was immense, in addition to the sacrifice which had been already made of silk, indigo, shell-lac, &c., thrown overboard, in order to make way for getting at the weightier portion of the cargo in the hurricane that prevailed. These ships were all, I believe, first-class; and if the severe shaking which they received was an accurate criterion as to the violence of the storm, Heaven only knows what became of our second-class vessels.

On this, as on similar occasions, I heard many theories, (various, ingenious, and plausible,) advanced on the Law of Storms, but none that in any way satisfied me as correctly defining the true principle. The general opinion seemed to be that the hurricane had caught the ships on its *recurve*, but no one could tell exactly how the masters of these vessels were to know when the hurricane *had recurved;* and it appeared to me, that for want of this essential knowledge, any mere abstract speculation upon the Law of Storms would be of little practical benefit. Again and again did reflections upon this matter recur to me, and, during my voyage homeward, my attention was constantly directed to it, as the recent disasters at the Mauritius had invested it with additional interest in my mind, and impressed it very vividly upon me.

Such are the circumstances which led, in the first instance, to the publication of the present treatise. I venture to hope that it may convey a more *practical* knowledge of the Law of Storms than most of the works that have hitherto been presented to the public, as it is with that view that I have written it.

In the works which have hitherto been published on the Law of Storms, rules are given by which the vortex of a hurricane may be avoided, when the tract assumed is somewhat near the right one; and, in illustration of this theory, it has been shown how a projection may be made for ascertaining the hurricane's track. But masters of vessels have frequently, for want of some definite rules to guide them on all occasions, run into the vortex of a storm when they might have avoided it. We have sufficient positive knowledge of the Law of Storms in both Hemispheres, to be aware that they travel from east to west, curving to the southward and S.E. in the Southern Hemisphere, and to the northward and N.E. in the Northern Hemisphere. On this supposition, I have endeavoured to show how a ship may avoid getting into danger; and I have also, with the aid of diagrams, laid down rules which I believe to be so simple, and at the same time so clear and comprehensive, as, I trust, to render it easy for all those in charge of vessels, to avoid the destructive influence of a hurricane.

Previous to publishing my treatise on so important a subject, I considered it desirable to obtain the dispassionate opinion of a man of scientific and practical attainments, and I accordingly submitted the work to Mr. Prior, whose abilities and discriminating powers are well known. From him I received the following gratifying letter :—

> " Dear Sir,—I have carefully perused your concise treatise on the 'Law of Storms.' It contains much valuable information in a condensed form. The rules you have prescribed for avoiding the vortex of a hurricane are more general in their application than any I have yet seen, and are so clearly illustrated by explanatory diagrams, as to be rendered perfectly intelligible to the most ordinary capacity. The work, I think, cannot fail to be duly appreciated and patronised by those for whose use it has been written.
>
> " I remain, &c., &c.,
(Signed)   " W. H. Prior,
" Late Examiner of Navigation to the Trinity
House, and Christ's Hospital.
>
> " To James Sedgwick, Esq."

This is a subject which may be made of the highest importance to the shipping interest of Great Britain, as well as to that of every other nation ; and I leave it to those who are qualified to form an impartial judgment in the matter, to say whether I have succeeded in giving a plain practical bearing to a true theory, so as to make it of use to all whom it may concern. Assuming my theory to be the correct one (of which I, myself, entertain no doubt), capable of supporting the test of time and experience, and of bearing the investigation of the scientific, whose attention I would respectfully invite to it,—I have endeavoured, in this little work, to render it ready and available to all who are entrusted with the charge of vessels. It is my earnest hope that the plain directions which it contains may serve, in some degree, as a guide to our navigators, and assist in preventing the recurrence of those disasters which are yearly desolating our seas, to the destruction of life and property.

J. S.

London, 1852.

THE LAW OF STORMS.

CHAP. I.

SOUTHERN HEMISPHERE.

WE will commence with the Southern Hemisphere, and suppose ourselves either outward, or homeward bound from India. The appearance of the weather is threatening, and the barometer falling; in short, there are all *those* indications which foreshadow the coming of a *storm*. If the wind is at south, the centre of the storm must bear east, and as this is a difficult point to comprehend clearly, from the circumstance of the vortex always bearing at right angles to the wind, a diagram is annexed (see Fig. 2), which will render this fact more apparent. Although we cannot immediately tell the direction the storm is taking, still, by carefully observing the way in which the wind veers, we shall soon be able to ascertain whether the ship is in the right, or left-hand semicircle of its course, and to act accordingly. That there may be no mistake as to the semicircles, we will call that the right, which is on the right-hand when looking towards the *probable* track of the hurricane; or, what is the same thing, when the back of the person is turned to that quarter where the centre of the hurricane bears, when the first wind is observed. If the first shift of wind now occur to the eastward, it follows that we are in the left-hand semicircle, and the ship ought to be brought to the wind on the port tack; and as the wind comes round, the vessel will bow the sea; by this means, the ship, although she may have to encounter a heavy gale, will avoid getting too near the vortex of the storm. But if the wind should shift to the westward, we shall then be in the right-hand semicircle, and as the wind will permit us to run, we should scud to the northward. Similar results will follow with the wind at S. b E.; SS.E.; S.E. b S.; S.E.; S.E. b E.; E.S.E; E. b S., and East. With the wind at E. b N. the centre of the hurricane will bear N. b W.; and whether it has commenced its recurve, or not, if the wind shift to the northward, it shows that we are in the left-hand semicircle, and that the ship ought to be on the port tack. But if the wind shift to the southward, it shows that we are in the right-hand semicircle, and ought to run to the westward:—the same result follows with the wind commencing at E.N.E.; N.E. b E., and N.E.

To make the subject more plain, full directions are attached to every article (see Fig. 1), showing how to act with a certain wind. But it must be borne in mind, that the lines running through the circles, although they show the general track of hurricanes in the Southern Hemisphere, are not intended to show that the hurricane is actually travelling on these lines, at the time it is encountered, but are merely placed there to point out *the bearing of the centre of the hurricane with a certain wind.* For instance, if the wind be at S.E., the centre of the storm bears N.E., but it is impossible to tell in what direction it may be travelling. Let us suppose that the first shift of wind takes place to the southward, we know then that we are in the right-hand semicircle, and the storm may be travelling SS.W. or SS.E. of our position; for it is evident that it cannot be travelling to the northward of our position, otherwise the wind would have shifted to the eastward of S.E. Had it done so, the ship ought to have been brought to the wind on the port tack; and in order to avoid getting too close to the vortex of the hurricane,

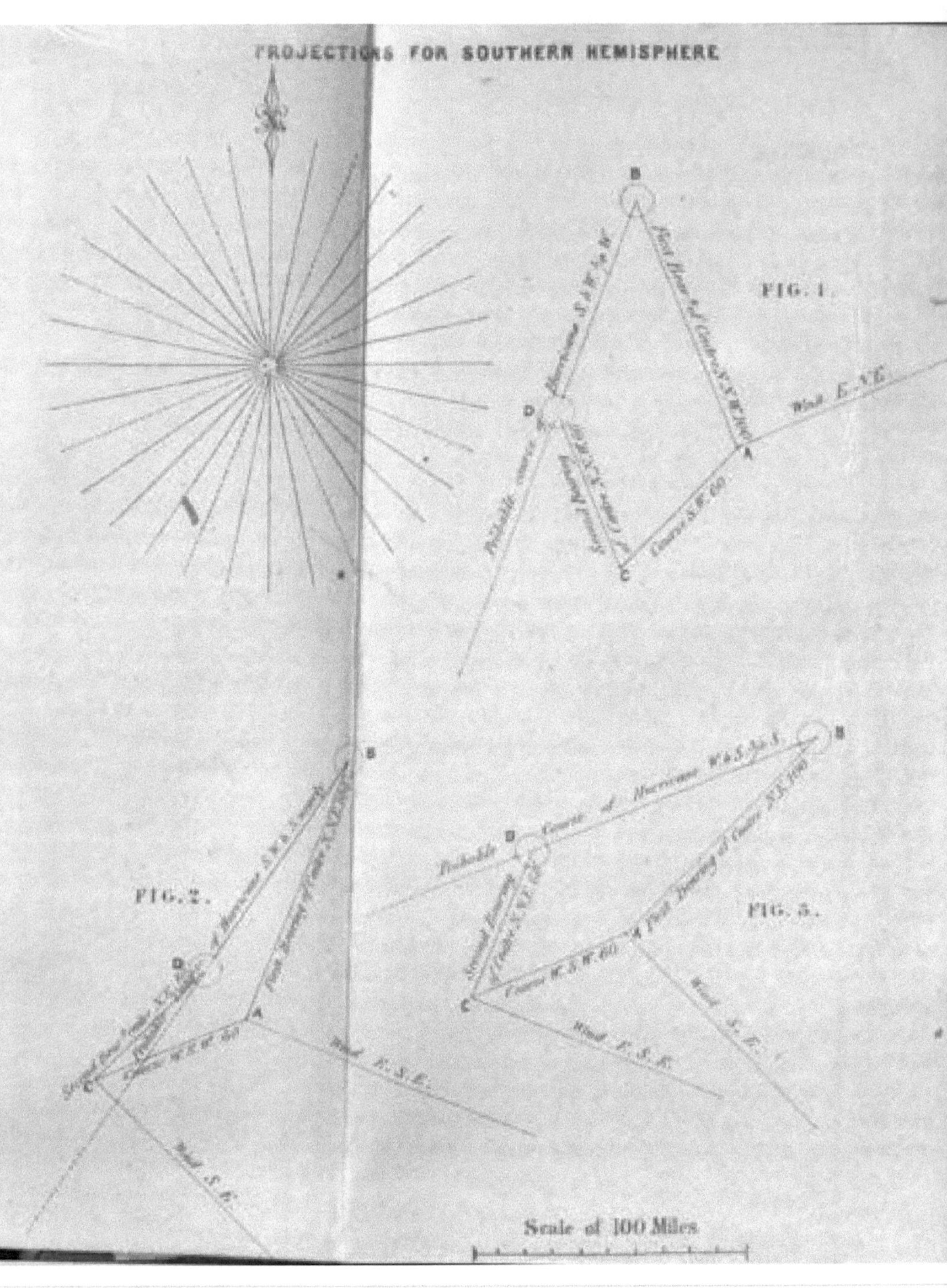
FIG. 1.
FIG. 2.
FIG. 3.
Wind E. N E.
Wind N. S. E.
Wind S. E.
Wind S. E.
Wind S. S. E.
Course S. E. 60
B
A
C
D
Scale of 100 Miles

it would be desirable to run to the S.E.: but the wind being from that quarter, renders it impossible for us to do so, and all that can be done is to make the ship as snug as possible by getting top-gallant masts on deck, preventer gaskets on yards, &c. ; in short, every precaution should be taken that the prudent seaman considers necessary at such a time ; this will probably save the masts, for on such occasions it is not in our power to say how far the vortex may pass clear of the vessel.

Getting near the vortex of a hurricane is so dangerous, and yet of such common occurrence to vessels. both outward and homeward bound from India, that I purpose pointing out how to act in a case where a ship may be overtaken by a storm. We will assume the ship's course to be W.S.W., say in about latitude 14°S. and longitude 80°E. (a ripe place for hurricanes); the wind blowing strong at S.E., and the barometer indicating bad weather. To be on the safe side it would be better to shorten sail, and round the ship to on the port tack ; if she is not in the track of a hurricane, a change of wind will soon occur ; and supposing the shift to take place to the eastward, the ship must be kept on the port tack, and pushed as long as sail can be carried to the southward ; but if the wind shift to the southward, we must run N.W. ; or, if the wind, after the ship has been rounded-to for five or six hours, increase rapidly without changing its direction, we must likewise run to the N.W., as the vortex of the storm is evidently approaching.

Fig. 2, is a diagram which shows that from whatever quarter a ship may have the wind, the vortex of a storm will bear at right angles to that wind. A hurricane may be compared to a whirlwind on a gigantic scale; and the wind set in motion on these occasions, may be likened to a coach-wheel revolving, whilst being cleaned; but with this difference, that as the outer edge of a coach-wheel appears to be turning round with inconceivable rapidity, when the barrel, or centre, is *apparently* turning round but slowly, so the wind in a hurricane, at its outer edge, is moving but slowly, when at or near the centre, it is *actually* blowing in circles with inconceivable velocity. As a hurricane in travelling must displace the ordinary trade wind, it seems probable that its outer edge would be very little stronger than the trade wind, but would collect as it advanced all the winds in its course, and give them circular motion; consequently, when a man asks, " *What am I to consider the first hurricane wind ?* " it seems safe to answer, that on indication of bad weather, he had better fall back to the time-when the wind was only unusually strong for the trade, especially if there has been a shift of wind since; this will give him correct data to act upon, and enable him to make a projection to show the probable course of the storm.

PROJECTIONS.

It has appeared to me useful to give a few projections, which are so simple, that let a man's mind be ever so much harassed at the idea of getting near the vortex of a hurricane, he will still find time to go below for five minutes and construct one. In this way he will be enabled, when any shift of wind takes place, to ascertain in which semicircle of the storm he is; and some degree of certainty will be given to the opinion he may form as to its probable course.

Fig. 1 shows a ship at A, with the wind at E.N.E. Consequently, the centre of the storm bears NN.W.; and as the lowest computation that can be given with reference to the distance of the ship from the centre of the storm, when she is enabled to run under single reefed top-sails, is 100 miles (or better still, it may be 150), a line drawn from where the ship is to the NN.W. quarter, and 100 miles being marked off to B, will show the nucleus of one of the most unpleasant things a man can well fall in with at sea. Suppose the ship to be running S.W., and going rapidly through the water, say ten knots an hour. In six hours she will have run sixty miles. Now, mark off sixty miles on a S.W. course; this brings the ship to C. During these six hours we must allow the hurricane to have travelled also, and as it is blowing harder, but still in the same quarter, the vortex of the hurricane must be nearer to us; we may call it twenty, forty, or sixty miles nearer; say forty miles, which taken from the first distance of 100 miles, leaves sixty miles, and as the wind is the same, the vortex of the hurricane must bear the same, but it is only sixty miles off. Now, lay sixty miles off from the second position of the ship at C, on a NN.W. line, which will reach to D; a line drawn from the two points of the bearing of the storm's centre, B D, shows the course of the hurricane to be about S. b W., three-quarters W.; and consequently the ship is running right across its track. There is still time to avoid it, if the vessel's head be put to the S.E.; but a very heavy brush of its tail will be felt in consequence of running so long.

Fig. 2 shows a ship at A, the wind at E.S.E.; consequently the centre of the hurricane bears NN.E.; and let the same distance be assumed, namely, 100 miles at B. (It matters little whether we call the distance 100 or 200 miles, the result will be the same.) Let us now suppose the ship to have sailed W.S.W. sixty miles to C, and we then find the wind has shifted to S.E., consequently at the point C, the centre of the hurricane must bear N.E.; and as the wind is now much stronger, we will say the distance is only sixty miles; a line from C to the second bearing of the centre of the storm, and sixty miles being marked off, shows the centre at D. Another line from the two bearings, B D (carried on), gives the probable course of the hurricane a little to the westward of S.W. by S., and it will be perceived that the ship has run into a very dangerous position, although she has got into the right hand semicircle, as the veering of the wind as well as the projection indicates. Now, to continue on this course would be wrong; for although you might escape the vortex, it would pass so near, that the loss of a few spars would seem inevitable. The ship's head should, therefore, be put at right angles to the storm's course, namely, N.W. b. W.

Fig. 3 shows a ship at A., the wind S.E., with the centre of the storm bearing N.E., the same distance off, namely, 100 miles at B. Suppose the ship to have sailed W.S.W. sixty miles. This places her at C; but instead of the wind shifting two points to the southward, as in the former projection, it has shifted two points to the eastward, and is now E.S.E.; the centre of the hurricane will bear NN.E., and as the wind has increased, it must be nearer, say only sixty miles off; this gives the centre of the hurricane at D, and a line drawn from B to D, shows the probable course of the hurricane, and indicates that if the ship be edged away to the southward, the centre of the storm will pass, and the course may be again resumed.

It will be seen that projections are of great utility when the distance run by the ship, after the first bearing of the storm has been taken, is considerable, especially if the wind continue in the same quarter, as the ship-master naturally feels very anxious to know on which side of the storm's track he is.

CHAP. II.

From the full, and at the same time concise instructions, which I have endeavoured to give for the guidance of those who may be exposed to the chance of a hurricane in the Southern hemisphere, I feel that there will be little difficulty in carrying out the same views with reference to the Northern hemisphere, where storms rage with equal violence in the Bay of Bengal, and in the West Indies, and, under the name of typhoons, in the China Sea.

It is a well-attested fact, that the rotatory motion of the wind in hurricanes in the Northern hemisphere is exactly the reverse of what it is in the Southern hemisphere, as it blows in circles from right to left, or, as sailors term it, goes round left-handed; but at the same time, the vortex of a hurricane will always be at right angles to the wind in either hemisphere, blow from what quarter it may.

The track of storms in the Northern hemisphere appears to be similar to the track pursued by those in the Southern hemisphere, coming from the east; but, instead of curving to the southward and S.E., they curve to the northward and N.E. With these few preliminary remarks, I will proceed to give instructions to avoid the vortex of a storm in the Northern hemisphere.

Fig. 1 shows the general track of hurricanes in the Northern hemisphere. If a hurricane be threatening, with the wind at north, the vortex must bear east; and as it is equally as impossible in the Northern as in the Southern hemisphere, to tell immediately the direction the storm is taking, we must

carefully observe the way the wind veers. If the first shift of
wind occur to the eastward, it shows the hurricane to be
travelling to the southward of our position, and that we are in
the right hand semicircle; consequently, as we cannot run to
the northward, we must lay-to on the starboard-tack ; but if the
shift of wind be to the westward, it shows the hurricane to be
travelling to the northward of our position ; and, as we are in
the left hand semicircle, we can run to the southward, so as to
get well clear of the vortex.

Rules are laid down in every circle, as in the Southern
hemisphere, to point out the way to act ; and I will give a case
which will answer either for the Bay of Bengal, China Sea, or
West Indies. Suppose a ship to be entering the range of a
hurricane with the wind at N.E. It follows that the centre will
bear S.E. ; and if those in charge of the vessel persist in running
down the Bay of Bengal, or China Sea, without first ascertaining
if they be in the right or left hand semicircle, it is very
probable that they may become overwhelmed in the vortex.
As the loss of four, five, or six hours is very trifling, or as the
result may show the delay to be a gain, I think none but a
madman would neglect rounding-to, for the purpose of ascertaining whether he was in the left or right hand semicircle of the
storm's track; and having taken this precaution, let him
round-to on the starboard-tack. If the wind now veer to
the eastward of N.E., he may rest satisfied with his position,
and feel assured that he will escape the vortex, as he is in the
right hand semicircle ; but he should be prepared for a heavy
gale. If the wind should shift to the northward of N.E., it
shows that he is in the left hand semicircle of the storm's track,
and may run to the S.W. But if, after laying-to for a considerable time, no shift of wind should occur, he may be certain
that he is nearly, if not quite, in the track of the vortex, and
ought to run S.W. At the same time, it must be admitted that
there is always some danger in this proceeding ; although, as a
choice of two evils, this is the least, since by running at right
angles to the storm's track. the vortex may be avoided. But by

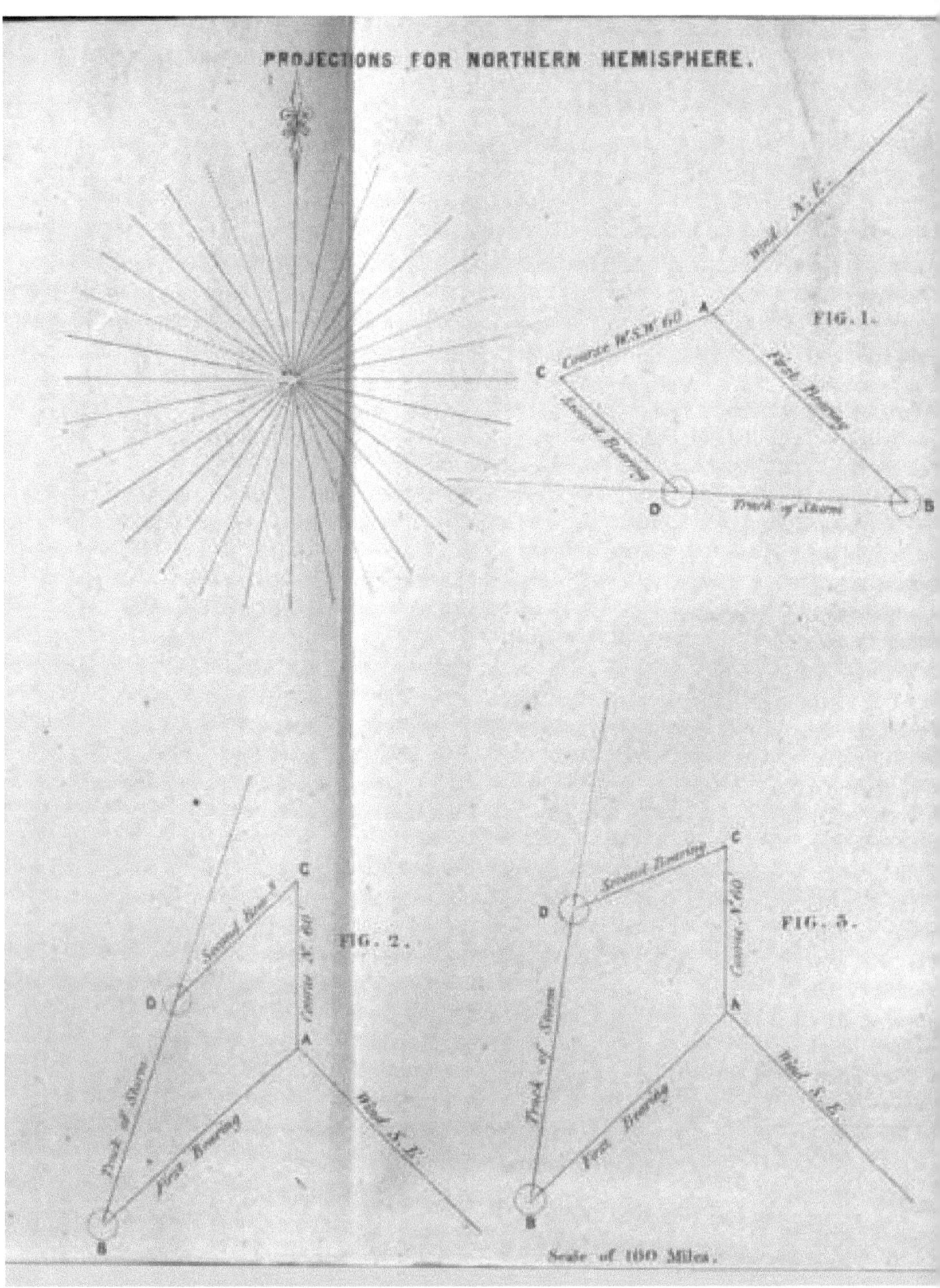
FIG. 1.
Wind N. E.
Course W.S.W. 60
A
First Bearing
C
Second Bearing
D
Track of Storm
B
FIG. 2.
C
Second Bearing
Course N. 60
D
A
Track of Storm
First Bearing
Wind S. E.
B
FIG. 3.
C
Second Bearing
D
Course N. 60
A
Track of Storm
First Bearing
Wind S. E.
B
Scale of 100 Miles.

laying-to, even under bare poles, and with top-gallant masts struck, the finest ship ever launched may become disabled.

PROJECTIONS.

A FEW projections are here introduced to assist the mariner in the Northern hemisphere. It will be perceived that I have avoided putting circles to the projections, in the Southern as well as in the Northern hemisphere, for I think they would only tend to confuse the learner; whereas the man who grasps the subject, as it were, will easily understand that he is within the range of large circles of wind, and that the vortices of those circles are only introduced into the projections, so as not to confuse the eye.

Fig. 1 shows a ship at A, with the wind at N.E., and with every indication that a storm is near. It follows that the centre must bear S.E., and we will say that it is 100 miles off. A line drawn from A to the S.E. quarter, and 100 miles laid off, shows the first bearing of the centre; the ship may be steering W.S.W., and after running sixty miles, find the wind increasing so rapidly, as to leave no doubt on the mind as to a hurricane raging in the vicinity; consequently, sixty miles on a W.S.W. course is laid off, which places the ship at C; the wind continuing from the same quarter, the vortex must bear the same, and as the wind is much stronger than it was when the first bearing was observed, we will suppose the vortex to be only sixty miles off, at D. A line drawn from B to D gives the probable track of the hurricane W. half N. and shows the vessel to be crossing its path.

Fig. 2 shows a ship at A, with the wind S.E.; the vortex of a storm will bear S.W., say 100 miles off at B. Now, if the ship run to the northward sixty miles to C, the vortex will bear the same; provided there be no shift; and supposing it to be only sixty miles off at this second bearing, it will be at D. A line drawn from B to D shows the probable track of the storm to be N. b E. half E., and crossing the track of the vessel;

it will, therefore, be prudent to round-to, and see which way the wind veers.

Fig. 3 shows a ship at A, with the wind at S.E.; the vortex consequently bears S.W., and the distance at B may be assumed at 100 miles. Now if the vessel sail north sixty miles to C, and it be found that, on arriving there, the wind has shifted to SS.E., the centre of the storm will then bear W.S.W. at D, which gives the track of the storm about N. half E.—and it is evident that if the vessel be hauled to the eastward for a short time, the storm will soon pass.

CHAP. III.

It is well ascertained that the wind in hurricanes blows in circles in both hemispheres; and whether the general. track laid down in this treatise be quite correct or not, the practical plan now shown, which supersedes the use of the hurricane card, and the necessity for assuming a track, will enable the mariner to ascertain how the nucleus of his enemy bears from him ; and the plain directions which I have given will also point out to him how to act. In the event of a deviation in the course taken by the hurricane, let him only keep his back to the vortex (which must always be at right angles to the wind), and any changes that may occur will soon apprise him if the storm be coming towards him, or going from him. It will be seen by the foregoing remarks, how unnecessary it would have been for me to have extended this treatise, by showing the mariner what steps to take with the wind having westing in it. I feel certain that there will be no practical difficulty in comprehending the subject which I have endeavoured to illustrate. A little attention will soon enable any one to form a correct idea of the manner in which he must act in the dangerous quadrant, and in all places of difficulty, where a deviation from the general track of the storm takes place.

In the two preceding chapters, I believe I have laid down correct rules, and made them sufficiently clear, to enable any man, who will give his mind to the subject, to avoid the centre of a storm. And now, as I have remarked that some seamen, when first they find themselves in the outer limits of a storm, imagine they can take their ships on either side of the storm's path, I will endeavour to show the error and fallacy of such an idea.

In the Southern hemisphere, with a S.E. wind, it was heretofore recommended to run N.W., without waiting to see which way the wind veered ; and with a N.E. wind, to stand to the southward, without reference to the shift. This, I need not say is the error which we have been committing for many years. Ships from India, after crossing the Equator, frequently get into the outer circles of a storm, with the wind at N.E. ; and to stand to the S.E. with the wind travelling in a S.E. direction would be madness indeed. With the wind at S.E., a ship may be in the left hand semicircle: will any practical seaman venture to assert that it would be better policy to make a dash to the N.W., and try to cross the storm's path ? The different writers on this important subject inform us that hurricanes sometimes travel from four to five miles an hour, and that, at other times, their velocity is as great as from twenty, thirty, to forty miles in the hour. Who, when within the outer limits of these *terrestrial meteors*, will attempt to guess his distance from the centre, and say, " I feel confident that this storm is one of the slow moving ones, and there will be time to get across its path " ? Surely, common sense will point out, that if the vessel be in the left hand semicircle with a S.E. wind in the Southern hemisphere, it is better to prepare for the worst, and to make up one's mind to a heavy gale. In such a case there can be no danger to a ship that is seaworthy ; for as the storm progresses, no matter with what velocity, the wind will draw aft, and the vessel consequently bows the dangerous sea.

This recommendation is intended for a time when the veering of the wind is so definite as to leave no doubt on the mind about the ship's position being in the left hand semicircle of the storm. But if the wind should " veer and haul " (as seamen term it), that is, change a point or two one way, then come back again, this shows that there is some oscillation, incurving, or turning of the entire body of the storm, and that its direction is nearly if not quite towards the ship. Under these circumstances, it would be better for a man to scud his vessel before the wind.

My impression is that the science of Meteorology is only in its infancy; and that discoveries will be made which astonish the sceptical in the same manner that steam, chronometers, and the method of avoiding storms which have proved so disastrous to our East India shipping, would make the long-tailed tars of last century open their eyes rather widely if they could pay us a visit from the shades.

I am a convert to Sir William Reid's opinion, that all winds are moving in circles. At the same time, I think that it is only in very strong winds that anything like a complete circle is formed;—and the reason of this, a little reflection will enable any one to understand. Air is elastic, and capable of being compressed; and as there may be hundreds or even thousands of circular bodies of air in motion around our globe, one body may press against another in such a manner as to give it a form anything but circular. But in the case of a violent wind, the surrounding currents of air (of which the motion could not be so strong) would naturally, in a greater or less degree, become involved into the larger storm. Wind, also, coming in contact with land, would have its circular motion impaired. Seamen can, therefore, avail themselves but little of the knowledge that all winds are circular, except in case of very strong winds, and away from land. Then, they may not only keep clear of the centre, but, in the event of getting into that part of the circle of wind which is contrary for the ship, a deviation in the course may be made so as to reach a circular vein of wind that is fair.

To enable my readers to understand more clearly what I mean, the following account of two strong gales in a high latitude encountered by me, may not be without interest:—

In latitude 39° S., longitude 23° E., my barometer fell from 30.10 to 29.40, and a gale commenced at NN.W. Ship's head S.E. b E. Close reefed the main topsail, double reefed the fore one, and scudded under these two sails, together with the foresail and fore top mast staysail. The barometer now fell to 29.08, and I expected something very severe, as this was unusually low for a high set barometer to fall, except when near the vortex of a tropical hurricane. However—and this fact is significant and important, and fully corroborates an idea which I have long entertained, that the low range of a barometer is not always a criterion for the strength of the wind likely to be encountered—in the present instance, the fall was caused by thunder and lightning, accompanied with violent squalls of rain, but not more wind than any ship of our size (800 tons) might scud under with double reefed topsails. I remarked that, during the squalls, the wind always came from N.W., and, after the squall was over, backed again to NN.W. I concluded from this, that the vessel was running on the same track as the storm, and that the backing of the wind was simply caused by oscillation or incurving. It was my wish to steer East, with a view to draw the ship a little to the northward of the storm's track, but being apprehensive that, with a NN.W. wind, this would bring the sea too much on the port beam, and not liking to run to the southward, I determined to brave the worst,—storms in high latitudes being seldom feared by seamen. I had occasion, however, to repent not taking more precaution; for, in a sudden squall, the wind shifted without the slightest notice to SS.W., and blew with equal violence, which compelled me to keep the ship E.N.E., while the foresail was being hauled up and the yards turned round. This shift of wind caused a tremendous sea to rise, and heavy lurching and rolling were, of course, a necessary accompaniment. Now, to younger men, who may wish to save themselves from having a clean sweep of their decks on some occasions, I will explain in what respect I was wrong. Having ascertained that I was travelling very nearly, if not quite, upon the same track as that on which the whole body of the storm was moving—which is easily done by projection,—I should have hauled either to the northward or southward, so as to get on one side of it; by which means, the shift of wind would not have been so sudden. For instance: the centre of the storm, with a NN.W. wind, was bearing W.S.W., and travelling to the southward of East; and had I altered the course to East, which might have been done by *conning* the man at the wheel a little, the ship would have been kept to the northward of the vortex,—the wind would have shifted, as the centre passed to N.W., West and S.W., but gradually,—and the sea would not have been so confused. On the other hand, had I altered the course to SS.E., and succeeded in getting across the storm's path, the wind would have shifted from NN.W. to North round by East. The centre of the storm having southing in its bearing, and travelling to the southward of East, the former plan (that of keeping on the northern side) would have been the best.

These observations are founded on facts; and any man who will take sufficient interest to understand the subject, will find it as simple as working a common day's reckoning.

On the next occasion on which I encountered a storm, I took the precaution to keep clear of the centre; and, by doing so, as the wind was contrary for the ship, the vessel was actually brought into a fair wind. The incredulous will, of course, laugh at such a notion; but I will undertake to prove that such was the case, with the same certainty that a problem in mathematics can be demonstrated. Let any seaman, who feels interested, take a parallel ruler, pencil, and pair of compasses; and having a compass roughly sketched, with a scale of miles of any convenient size at the lower edge of a sheet of paper, proceed as follows:—

The barometer having fallen very suddenly to 29.40, indicated an approaching storm;—the wind was E.S.E. Now place the parallel ruler over the E.S.E. point of the compass, and draw a line; another line, drawn from this at right angles, or in the NN.E. direction, will show the first bearing of the storm's centre; and the distance we will assume as 100 miles, which can be marked off from the scale at the foot of the paper. (It is of no importance whatever whether we assume 100 or 300 miles, as it will amount to the same thing, or nearly so, in proving the track of the storm.) The vessel having sailed with an increasing wind twenty miles in a N.E. b N. direction, another line must be drawn to the N.E. b N. from the point at the right angle formed by the two lines already made, and twenty miles must be marked off from the same scale from which the first bearing of the storm's centre was taken. Having run these twenty miles, the wind now shifted a point and a half to the southward, and another line must be drawn to S.E. ½ E. from the ship's position after running the twenty miles; a line now drawn at right angles from the one which shows the wind, will give the second bearing of the storm's centre N.E. ½ E.; and as the wind is stronger, the centre must be nearer, say seventy miles off. From the second bearing, the ship sailed N.E. twenty-five miles; and on arriving at this point, the wind was SS.E., which gave the third bearing of the storm's centre E.N.E. The topsails by this time were double reefed, and as the storm was coming thick and fast, we may assume the centre as not being more than forty-five miles off. A line now drawn through the three points representing the bearings of the centre of the storm, will show the storm's track to be nearly S.E. b S. (It may be as well here to state that however much men may disagree in their distances with regard to the centre, this will not alter the track of a storm more than a point either way. For instance: suppose I had assumed the distance of the storm's centre at the first bearing as 150 miles, and the distance at the second bearing as 100 miles, the track of the storm would have been about SS.E.) At 5 p.m. the wind increased so rapidly, that I remarked to the chief officer,—" We are in the right hand semicircle of a severe storm, and must do one of two things,—either lay to under a close reefed main topsail, and brave the worst, for the centre cannot pass over us,—or run the ship out of her course to get away from it, and haul up as much as we can as the wind veers round." I chose the latter plan; although I did not expect, at the time, that we should have been enabled to resume our course so soon as we did. At 5 p.m., squared the yards, and steered North,— wind SS.E.

There are perhaps few seamen who would run eight points

from their course to look for a better wind; and before condemning such a proceeding hastily, I trust they will pause and reflect upon the case, and then decide whether the step I took was not politic and rightly judged. My officers were incredulous until they saw the result; when the second officer, who was on deck with me in the middle watch, exclaimed (to use his own words),—" Well, I have been to sea thirty years, and I never saw such a clever thing done before, but I cannot understand it."

After bearing up, the storm increased rapidly, and from 8 p.m. to $9\frac{1}{2}$ p.m., the gusts were terrific; the wind appeared to come, not in an horizontal direction, but downwards, as if the Genii of all the winds were collected immediately above our heads, and expending their utmost fury in an effort to do us some damage. It was impossible to stand without holding on to something, and almost impossible to steer the ship. Two men, however, did succeed in keeping her before the wind; and I felt convinced that every mile the ship ran would take us farther away from the lion's jaws. At 10 p.m., the wind shifted to South, and the gusts were less violent; hauled up NN.E. At 11 p.m., wind SS.W. and moderating, hauled up N.E. At midnight, the dark gloom which had enveloped us began to clear a little ; hauled up E.N.E. ; wind moderating fast. At 1 a.m., the moon, at the first quarter, seemed inclined to show her mild cheering countenance, and the wind having shifted to S.W., we hauled up East, and finally E. b S.

Those who may have given these details their attention, will have perceived that the wind shifted, upon an average, a point every hour; but if the vessel had been laid-to with her head to the Eastward, the shift of wind—although it would have been in the same direction, the ship being to the Northward of the storm—would have been more sudden as the centre passed, and would probably have caused some damage in consequence of the confused sea. What surprised me more than the shift of wind, was the absence of any swell to give the ship a pitching motion, when the course was altered from

North to E. b S., as only eight hours had elapsed from the time when the vessel was kept North and it was blowing a violent tempest, till the proper course was resumed. The only way in which I can account for it, is by presuming that the storm was of small extent, probably covering a diameter of not more than 150 miles. The frequent changes of wind will also be explained on this supposition, as it will show that the ship was not very far away from the centre of the storm when she was first kept before the wind.

I have cited these examples as illustrations from my own personal experience, thinking that they may perhaps throw additional light upon my view of the Law of Storms, and bring home more clearly to my brother seamen the practical working of the rules which I have laid down. I am not aware that there is anything further, at present, that I can add: and I shall, therefore, close these pages by repeating my earnest hope that my little book may prove, at times, a useful companion and guide to the mariner in the emergencies of which it treats.

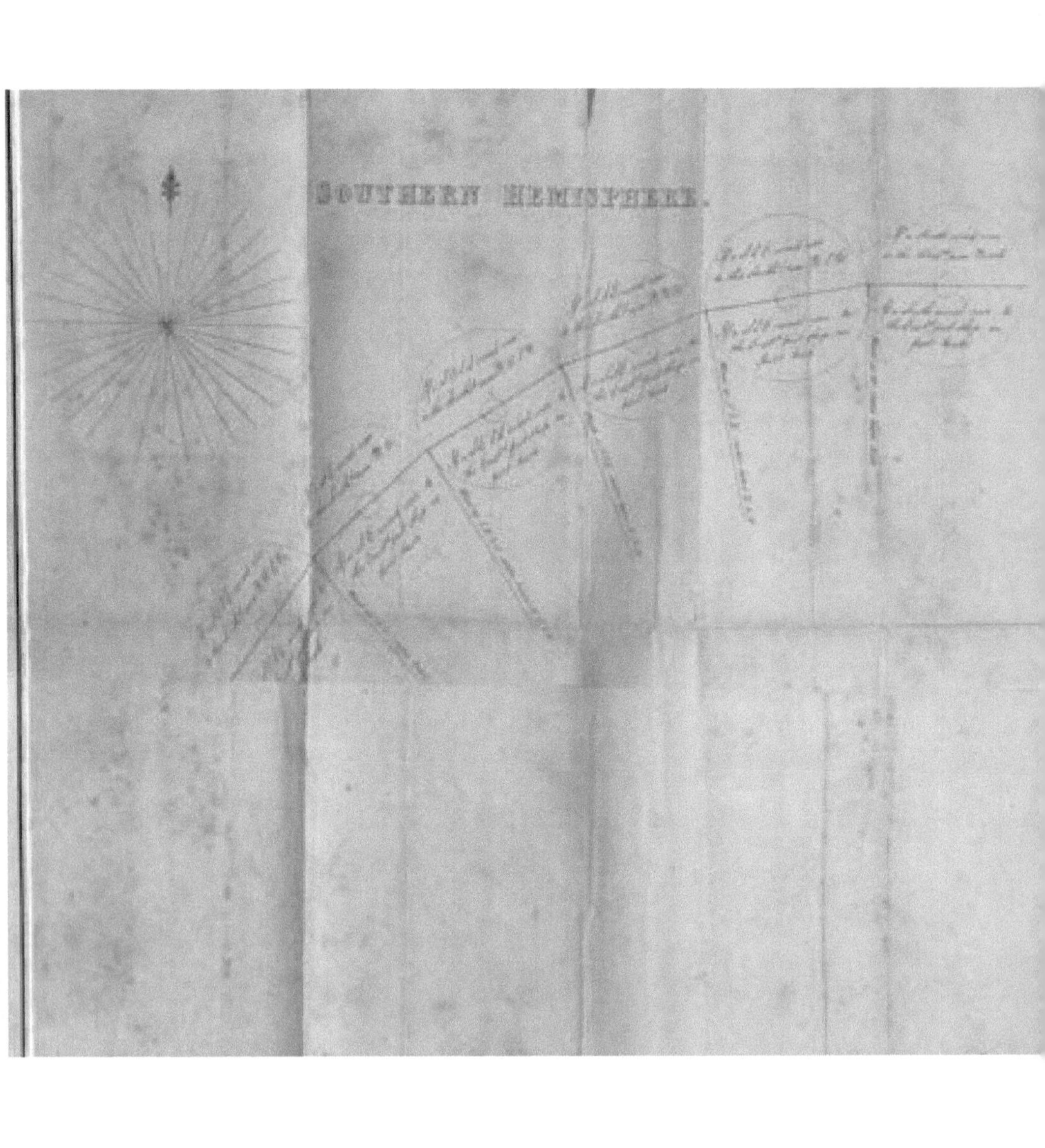

SOUTHERN HEMISPHERE.

Explanation of Diagrams in the Southern Hemisphere.

Fɪɢ. 1 is intended to represent the bearing of the vortex of a hurricane, in every wind from which danger to a ship may be apprehended, in the Southern Hemisphere ; so that those in charge of vessels, conversant with this scheme, will ha' e no difficulty in applying it, as it supersedes the use of the hurricane card, and the necessity for assuming a track ; in short, it shows those, " whose business is in the great waters," the way to avoid danger, whether the hurricane has recurved or not.

Fig. 2 is a diagram representing the manner in which the wind is perpetually revolving in a hurricane in the Southern Hemisphere ; and a glance will show that, whether on the north, south, east, or west side of the storm, whatever wind may be blowing, the centre of the storm must bear at right angles, and this forms the basis by which is demonstrated the theory in Fig. 1.

Fig. 3 further corroborates the theory, showing that a ship at A, getting the wind at east, must have the vortex bearing north ; if the wind now shift two points to the southward, this shows that the hurricane cannot be travelling south, but must be going, to the eastward of south, as the vortex will bear NN.E. Consequently, a ship can run with safety ; but if the wind shift two points to the northward of east, *this also shows that the hurricane* cannot be travelling south, but must be going to the westward of south, as the vortex will bear NN.W?, and the ship must lay to on port tack.

It may be objected that a ship has motion as well as a hurricane, but a little reflection will easily tend to obviate such objection, when it is remembered that the drift of a ship is not greater than a knot and a-half an hour, a mere trifle in comparison with the rate at which a hurricane travels ; if the ship be running, then a *projection* may be used with advantage, and the two combined will give a certainty to the conclusion at which those in charge of ships may arrive.

Explanation of Diagrams in the Northern Hemisphere.

FIG. 1 is similar to the figure in Southern Hemisphere, with this difference, that instead of recurving to the southward, and S.E., it recurves to the northward, and N.E.

Fig. 2 is a diagram representing the manner in which the wind is perpetually revolving in a hurricane in the Northern Hemisphere—the reverse way to what it does in the Southern Hemisphere—but notwithstanding, the wind will always be at right angles to the vortex of the storm, whichever side of a storm the ship may be on.

Fig. 3 corroborates the theory as in the Southern Hemisphere, showing that a ship at A, getting the wind at east, must have the vortex of a hurricane bearing south, and if the wind should shift two points to the southward, this shows that the hurricane cannot be travelling north, but must be going to the westward of north, as the vortex will bear SS.W. Consequently, as it would be folly to attempt to cross the hurricane's track, or even sail in company with it, the ship must be hove to, on starboard tack ; but if the shift of wind had taken place to the northward, then the hurricane would have been travelling somewhere to the eastward of north, and the vessel could run with safety to the westward.